First Facts™

Health Matters

Colds

by Jason Glaser

Consultant:
James R. Hubbard, MD
Fellow in the American Academy of Pediatrics
Iowa Medical Society
West Des Moines, Iowa

Capstone
press

Mankato, Minnesota

First Facts is published by Capstone Press,
151 Good Counsel Drive, P.O. Box 669, Mankato, Minnesota 56002.
www.capstonepress.com

Library of Congress Cataloging-in-Publication Data
Glaser, Jason.
    Colds / by Jason Glaser.
    p. cm.—(First facts. Health matters)
    Summary: "Introduces readers to the common cold, its symptoms, treatments, and
prevention"—Provided by publisher.
    Includes bibliographical references and index.
    ISBN 0-7368-4289-6 (hardcover)
    1. Cold (Disease)—Juvenile literature. I. Title. II. Series.
RF361.G56 2006
616.2'05—dc22   2004031051

Editorial Credits
Mari C. Schuh, editor; Juliette Peters, designer; Kelly Garvin, photo researcher/photo editor

Photo Credits
BananaStock Ltd., 15
Capstone Press/Karon Dubke, cover (girl), 8, 9, 10, 11, 14, 20 (bowl), 21
Corbis/Ariel Skelley, 12–13; Richard Gross, 6–7
Getty Images Inc./Gabrielle Revere, 5 (inset); Hulton Archive, 20;
    Steve Niedorf Photography, 16–17
Image Source/elektraVision, 1
Photo Researchers Inc./Dr. Steve Patterson, cover; Science Photo Library/Ian Boddy, 19
Visuals Unlimited/Dr. Gary Gaugler, 5

1 2 3 4 5 6 10 09 08 07 06 05

Table of Contents

What Is a Cold?

A cold is an illness caused by a **virus**. A virus is a tiny germ. It enters your body through your mouth or nose. Once inside, the virus copies itself over and over again. The viruses attack your body. As your body fights back, you feel sick. You start to show signs of a cold.

Fact!
More than 200 different kinds of viruses cause colds.

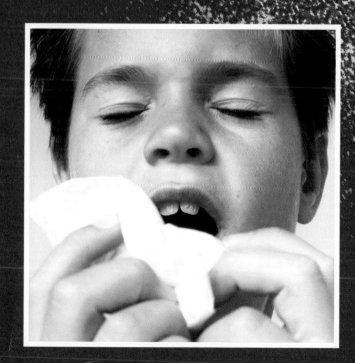

cold virus

5

Signs of a Cold

A common sign of a cold is a runny or stuffy nose. People with colds often sneeze and cough.

Colds also have other signs. People feel tired. Colds can cause sore throats and headaches.

Fact!
Most colds happen between early fall and late winter.

How Do Kids Get Colds?

Sneezing and coughing spread colds. The virus can get on your hands. Then the virus can spread to whatever you touch.

Your friend can pick up a virus by touching what you touched. He may touch his mouth, nose, or eyes. Then the virus gets inside his body.

What Else Could It Be?

Signs of a cold may be signs of a different illness. The **flu** causes **fever** and makes the body hurt. Strep throat makes throats feel scratchy.

Allergies cause runny noses and sneezing. Allergies are reactions to things like dogs or dust. When these things are gone, sneezing usually stops.

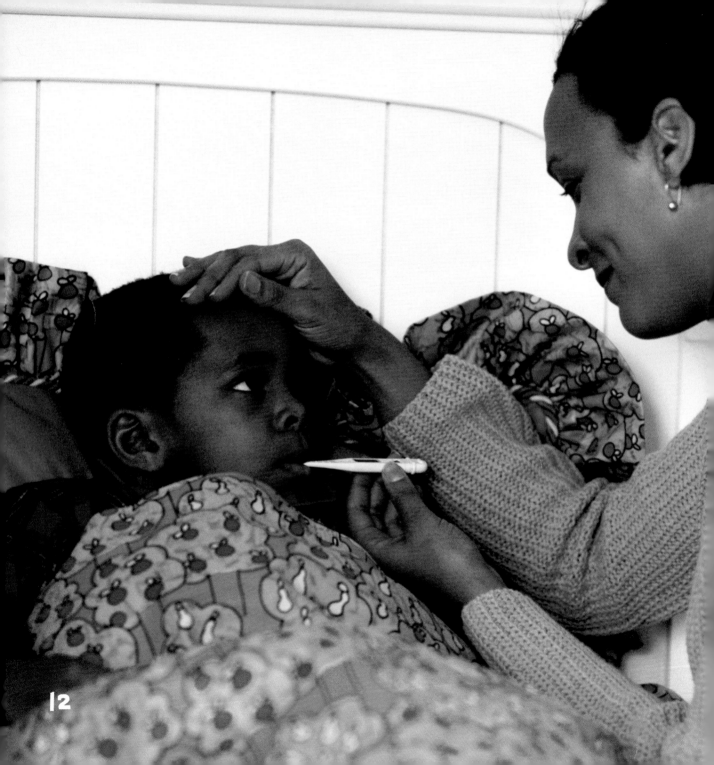

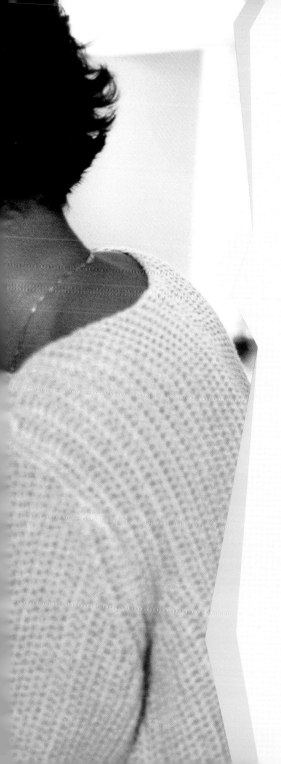

Should Kids See a Doctor?

Kids with colds usually don't need to see a doctor. Their bodies often stop cold viruses in about a week. Kids should see a doctor if a cold lasts longer than 10 days. High fevers also need a doctor's care.

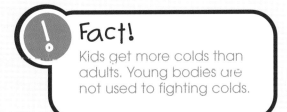

Fact!
Kids get more colds than adults. Young bodies are not used to fighting colds.

How to Treat a Cold

Rest and food can help the body fight a cold. Kids with colds need lots of sleep. Chicken soup and hot tea help the body fight colds.

14

Other things treat the signs of colds. Cold **medicine** may help stop coughing. **Gargling** salt water makes a sore throat feel better.

If It Gets Worse

Sometimes a person's body has a hard time fighting a cold. A bad cold can cause an earache or a bad sore throat. Some colds move into a person's lungs. Breathing becomes painful. People need to see a doctor when colds get worse.

Fact!
Medicine can make you feel better, but no medicine can cure a cold.

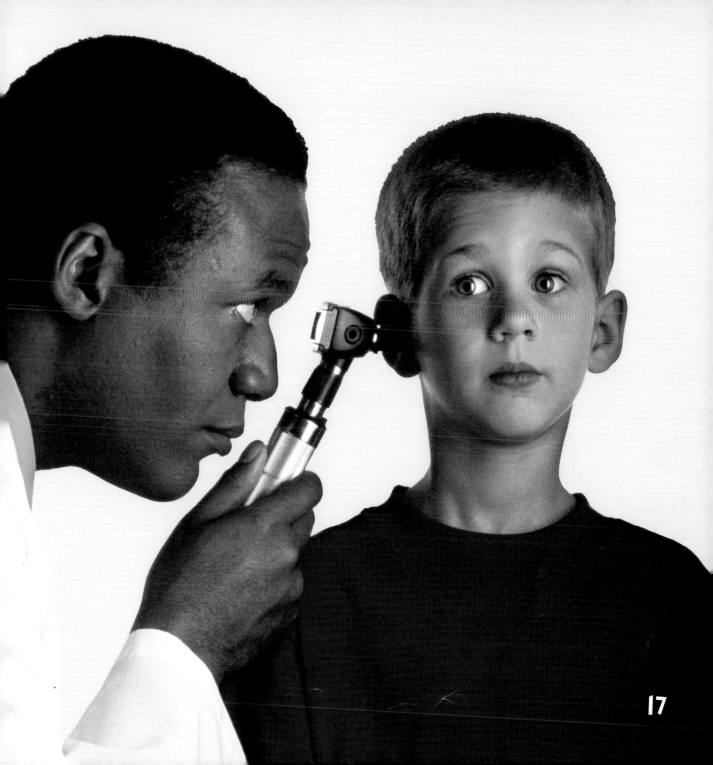

Staying Healthy

Washing your hands with soap and water can kill cold viruses. People may avoid colds by washing their hands and faces often.

Taking care of yourself protects you from colds. Eating fruits and vegetables keeps your body strong. Enough sleep makes your body ready to fight viruses.

Fact!
Some cold viruses can live outside the human body for many hours.

19

Amazing but True!

Chicken soup has been used to treat colds for a long time. A famous doctor named Maimonides (mye-MAHN-ee-deez) lived more than 800 years ago. He gave chicken soup as medicine to an Egyptian king named Saladin.

Maimonides

Hands On: Soapy Hands

Some illnesses can be spread by dirty hands. Have an adult help you with this activity.

What You Need

cooking oil	one friend
cinnamon	sink
measuring spoons	soap
adult helper	

What You Do

1. Rub one tablespoon (15 mL) of cooking oil on your hands. Have your friend do the same.
2. Sprinkle one teaspoon (5 mL) of cinnamon all over your hands. Have your friend do the same.
3. Wash your hands thoroughly for 20 seconds with warm water and soap.
4. Have your friend wash his or her hands thoroughly for 20 seconds with cold water and no soap.

Whose hands had less cinnamon on them? The cinnamon is like germs on people's hands. If you don't wash your hands well enough, germs can stay on your hands. Germs that are left on your hands can spread to other people.

Glossary

allergies (AL-er-jees)—reactions to things like dogs, cats, and dust; allergies cause runny noses, sneezing, and watery eyes.

fever (FEE-vur)—a body temperature that is higher than normal

flu (FLOO)—an illness that includes fever and muscle pain; flu is short for influenza.

gargle (GAR-guhl)—to move a liquid around in the back of your throat without swallowing it

medicine (MED-uh-suhn)—pills or syrup that can make people feel better during an illness

virus (VYE-ruhss)—a germ that copies itself inside the body's cells

Read More

Isle, Mick. *Everything You Need to Know about Colds and Flu.* Need to Know Library. New York: Rosen, 2000.

Royston, Angela. *Colds.* It's Catching. Chicago: Heinemann, 2002.

Silverstein, Alvin, Virginia Silverstein, and Laura Silverstein Nunn. *Common Colds.* My Health. New York: Franklin Watts, 1999.

Internet Sites

FactHound offers a safe, fun way to find Internet sites related to this book. All of the sites on FactHound have been researched by our staff.

Here's how:
1. Visit *www.facthound.com*
2. Type in this special code **0736842896** for age-appropriate sites. Or enter a search word related to this book for a more general search.
3. Click on the **Fetch It** button.

FactHound will fetch the best sites for you!

Index